Autographed Pag

2

DOUBLE
STANDARD

3

4

DOUBLE
STANDARD

DEBORAH J. BROADY

Double Standard

Copyright © 2015
Deborah J. Broady

Printed in the United States of America

Library of Congress – Catalogued in Publication Data

ISBN 978-0692523322

Published by:
Jabez Books Writers' Agency
(A Division of Clark's Consultant Group)
www.clarksconsultantgroup.com

Jabez Books

8

Dedication

This book is dedicated to my brilliant masterminded talented son, Fhedale A. Wallace (T Flow). He is not only filled with new and interesting ideas, but he is a talented artist, who is gifted with making music. He gave me one of his ideas to share with the world. God gave it to him and Fhedale shared it with me. Now, we get to release the idea to the world. If it wasn't for God, you, and my son, I don't know where I would be. Live your dream, my son. I love you.

Acknowledgements

Thank you to Desiree Greer (my daughter), for your support and encouragement; beautiful job, baby! And to Veronica Corona, greatest friend guardian angel; and to Harvest Church in Riverside, Fhedale Wallace, and Regina D. Taylor, for giving me the gift of God at a very young age. Harold Vanarsdale, Minister at a Church in Texas. Dan Sii, Inspirational counseling. Kevin and Marilyn Broady, you were always there for me. Devin Orange, greatest son ever! Dr. Shirley Clark, Minister and owner of Jabez Books. And God...I will forever acknowledge You!

Special Tribute

In life, most of us have gone through trials and tribulations. Sometimes we are overwhelmed by them. Sometimes we are able to navigate through them by ourselves. Other times, we need help to make it through. When people come into our lives to assist us to make changes in our lives, we might not always receive it at first, but I have learned over time, it just might be what we need or what we have been praying for. This is what God has done for me with my sister, Regina Taylor. God has used Regina to be an encouragement to me in my darkest moments. Her words of wisdom and counsel provided the support I needed to make it through. When I followed her counsel, my life began to change for the best. I became more focused and more positive things began to happen in my life. I will forever be grateful to my sister,

Regina, for allowing God to use her to bless my life. I love you, Sis, with all my heart!

Table of Contents

Chapter One: T Flow   15

Chapter Two: Pain   31

Chapter Three: Love At First Sight   43

Chapter Four: Jealous   53

Chapter Five: Blackout   71

Chapter Six: Record Contract   83

Chapter Seven: Moving Out   107

Chapter Eight: Engagement   145

Chapter Nine: Double Standard   165

Chapter One

T FLOW

As far back as I can remember, I was living in a house and everywhere I went, there were two of everything. In the bathroom, there were two step stools and two toothbrushes. In the bedroom, there were also two beds.

When clothes were brought for me, they were bought in sets of two. I guess it must have been buy one get one free or maybe I played so hard that I would wear out my clothes that a second set of clothes was needed in order to keep me clean and neat.

I also remember a man and a woman. Whenever they were around, I would have such a warm feeling inside.

I recall one night, when I was about three years old, the lady was looking very pretty all dressed up in this beautiful silk dress. I remember walking over to her and touching the nylons on her leg. She looked down at me on the floor, then she picked me up and kissed me on the cheek. Right after this, the man kissed me too.

"Gimme five," he said. Then the doorbell rang as I slapped his hand. When he opened the door, standing on the other side of the door was a lady who always played with me. She would bathe me, read me stories, and tuck me into bed at night when the man and woman were gone.

Also, she would stay in my room with me at night, but in the morning when I woke up, she would be gone. But the man and the woman would be asleep in another bedroom down the hall. I would crawl in the bed deliberately waking them up.

One night the woman and the man left and never came back. But when I woke up that morning, the lady who would read bedtime stories to me was still asleep in my bed.

When I first opened my eyes, I was scared. I ran to jump in the bed where I felt safe with the woman and man. However, they were not there this time. I started to cry. Then I woke up the lady who was in my bed sleeping. She too started to cry.

A few days later, a lot of people came over to the house. Everybody had on black, including myself as if we were at a funeral. All the people were eating and drinking. There were all sorts of food – chicken, macaroni & cheese, corn, ham, etc. Everything looked good.

Every time people would pick me up; they started crying as though I was ugly. So when these people put me down, I would run back to the people who were smiling and laughing.

After that day was over, I was resting in bed, but I could still hear my Granny talking.

"I will raise my little T Flow, but that is about all I can do right now." She said. Granny packed all my clothes in big brown cardboard boxes. I remember her packing my clothes and selecting only one outfit of each. Not knowing why she did this, so I went behind her and packed the identical pair.

She kept saying, "No, T Flow. We just have room for one, okay?" I still would sneak and pack my second pair. I knew she was not doing it right.

In between packing, she would take breaks and go downstairs to cry. I remember going and sitting on Granny's lap wiping her tears away and telling her not to cry.

First, I would run in the room and pack up my clothes the way she was supposed to have done it. I would think to myself, "What if I get dirty? I need two of them -- always two."

Granny's house was not as big as the house I was living in at the time. I still had a warm feeling in her home as though it was my own because she knew how to keep the laughter and smiles around me.

When I graduated from kindergarten, I led the class in the Star Spangled Banner song. When Granny picked me up from school that day, she cried. She said, "Your mommy and daddy would be so proud of you."

I looked at her and said, "Granny, I told the kids and my teacher that you are my mommy. They know I call you

Granny and I don't know where my daddy is."

Granny kissed me and took me home. She showed me a picture of a man and a woman. I was very surprised because I remembered these two people.

She said, "This is your mommy and daddy."

I choked up and started crying. "Granny, where are they?" I asked. "Do they not like me? Was I a bad boy?"

"No, No, No," she said. Then Granny grabbed a very special book off the shelf. It was a Bible. She started reading it to me. She told me that the Bible would make it so much easier for me to understand the things that happen in the world.

Right after this, Granny took me to a gravesite at least twice a year. She told me, this is where my mommy and daddy were buried.

There was no set time that we went to the gravesite, but from time to time, she would take me to it. I would lay my blanket on my parents' gravesite and fall asleep as Granny would pray and talk about me.

As I grew older, I would go to the gravesite on my own and talk to my mom and dad. I would share little secrets with them. I would even mention to them things that I did not tell Granny. I learned to not tell Granny everything because she never took me seriously. She would think I was just trying to get her attention. Life certainly changed and was different living with

my Granny.

Chapter Two

PAIN

"Granny, Granny, I have a pain in my side." This is what I hollered coming down the stairs. I was having sharp pains in my side that would not go away. It just "hit" me all of a sudden while lying in bed one day

33

upstairs in my room. It was a pain like someone had just slugged me as hard as they could. So I ran to tell Granny how bad I was hurting. Why did I do this? She immediately gave me some Pepto-Bismol medicine. She must have thought I liked the taste of Pepto-Bismol, but I didn't. I would have rather taken something else like Tums. Regardless, it did not take the pain away, so I went back and laid in bed until the pain actually went away.

34

Eventually, I feel asleep. When I woke up, the pain was gone. I was so glad that I was feeling better. In fact, I began to dance because I was feeling that great.

You see, I was always in my room dancing and trying to sing. I thought I was good, at least all of my friends and family used to tell me this.

However, when I was at school, I tried not to sing unless we were in our singing class because other kids would make fun of me. I thought they were just jealous because I was always chosen as the head leader in our Christmas singing programs. Heck, I even sang one song all the way through. They just sang the chorus. Yep, those kids were so jealous; especially, when they saw me wooing the crowd and I got a standing ovation. From that day forward, I loved being on stage. I was only ten years old.

During my adolescent years, there was one person that I would see at school, and we would pass ugly looks back and forth to each other before we actually became friends.

He was taking keyboard lessons. I hated to hear him play. He had no beat or rhythm. One day, he was playing so loud it got on my "last nerve." I was trying to study for a big math test and his awful playing was disrupting my concentration.

I walked two houses down from my house where he was playing. He was in the garage with the door up. He must have gotten a more advanced keyboard. As soon as I approached him, I said, "Man. That's tight!"

"You like it?"

"No doubt." I was all over his keyboard.

"Try it," he said.

I asked, "Ya sure?"

"Yeah. Can you play?"

"I bet I can play a beat better than you and I didn't even have to take lessons." It took me a minute to find a beat. When I finally found one, I started singing with my beat. Then I gradually grabbed his hand so he could play the beat as I took the microphone and got "busy." Then we started bouncing around, up and down and clowning. We were making "music." Then his parents came out to watch us perform. We could have done this all night long. But I realized I had to get back to my homework.

My neighbor Speed, who would later became my friend, started to pick up on a beat fast. He went from awful to great. Well, I can't give him all the credit because I would play with him until we came up with a beat together. We became so good in producing great sounds that we started entering talent contests.

One of the contests we entered when we were in junior high school, we won first place. And after that, we were offered all kinds of places to sing at. We became better and better. When we got to high school, we had our share of attention from the ladies. They would not leave us alone. We would be in class and girls would be daunting over us like they were in love. I never gave any of them the time of day. I was polite, but just not interested. My buddy Speed, had one or two girls hanging around almost every night. He loved the attention he got. However, I did not meet the girl of my dreams until my senior year in high school.

Chapter Three

LOVE AT FIRST SIGHT

DEBORAH J. BROADY

44

I never knew life could be so sweet until I met the girl of my dreams. It seemed as though the whole world opened up to me. She didn't go to the same school that I went to, so she didn't know anything about me or

Speed. I would never forget the moment I saw her.

It was in a restaurant called, "Desiree's Kitchen" that I saw her for the first time in my life. It was early one morning as Speed and I were on our way to school. We were both hungry, so we stopped to get something to eat. When we sat down, a waitress came and gave us a menu. This waitress said to us, "My shift is over but someone will be here to take your order in just one minute."

I was focused on the menu when the waitress arrived.

She took Speed's order first. Then she said in the most soft tone, "And you, Sir; what will you be ordering today?"

Still looking at my menu, I said, "I just can't decide. The number two looks good, but I like number five. So maybe I will just take both of them."

She said, "Are you sure? That's a lot of food."

I chuckled and said still looking at the menu and grabbing the menu to pass it to her, "Yep, baby, I put it away."

As I handed her the menu, I finally looked up at her. When I did, I couldn't take my eyes off of her. I felt like I went into somewhat of a trance for a moment. Before she left the table, I said, "Excuse me. What did you say your name was?"

She replied, "Melissa. I will be right back with your drinks."

The way that she looked at me told me I might just have a chance. However, she didn't give me the time of day. But there was no way that I was going to give up.

I would pass "Desiree's Kitchen" every day and I would wait to get her attention to wave hello and she would wave back. I wasn't hungry every day, so I did not get a chance or have a reason to go inside. However, all it took was for Melissa to give me a little bit of eye contact and I was in there. And I went inside the day she made eye contact with me. I wasn't even prepared for it. No man could pass that up.

I sat down at the table. She came up and asked me, "Can I take your order?"

"Uh, yes. I would like to order you."

She said, "But I am not on the menu."

"Can you be on my menu tonight?"

"That depends."

"I would show you a really nice time tonight. Can I please take you out tonight?"

She slid her number to me as she walked away and said, "We can talk about it."

As I walked out of the restaurant, I looked backed at her. I knew I was going to do everything in my power to make this girl mine.

Every night, I would talk to her on the phone, but she would not let me take her out. Instead, we got to know each other over the phone. You better believe it. I was just happy to have her on the telephone.

Chapter Four

JEALOUS

Boy, how things changed during those days. As Melissa and I were bonding more and more, Speed and our music were getting better also. We were singing in night clubs almost every night. Due to our busy schedule,

Melissa started getting a little jealous. I could hear it in her voice as I was talking to her one day.

"You work in a night club and you're only 18?" She asked this in a subtle disdain.

"Yep. You're right. I would be honored if you would let me take you to the place I work at."

She thought about it for a moment and then she said, "You know what? Okay. I'll go!"

"What? I mean, really?"

"Yep. I'll go. What time?"

"I can come pick you up."

"Yes. I want to go."

I really couldn't believe what I was hearing. I finally got this girl to give me a date. It was going to be where I work at though. So I knew I had to make it special. I sat down with Speed all night trying to find the right words to sing to this girl. By morning, we were ready.

I went to her door with the prettiest smelling flowers in the shop. I wanted to make a grand impression, so I got her a boutique of various colors of wildflowers. It was beautifully arranged. The response I was hoping for, I got.

Melissa loved the flowers and hugged me as a result of giving them to her. She looked so pretty that night. I just wanted to take her in my arms, but I knew I better not "blow" this date. The only thing I worried about was pulling up in the front of the club instead of the back, but security handled it very well.

The minute I got out the car, girls were screaming. Security helped us get inside safely. Melissa asked, "What is all the excitement out there?"

I calmly said, "It's always something going on out here."

I took Melissa to the back and introduced her to everyone that was in the room — my assistants, the musicians, the technical crew, and the other wives and girlfriends that were in the room.

However, I didn't take her to my dressing room. I had a special table set up just for her. Once I knew the guests were in the club, I knew it was time to perform. I asked security to assist Melissa to her table and I assured her, I would be right out.

I heard my introduction and came out on stage into a cloud of smoke as the music was playing. When the smoke disappeared, she was starring right at me grinning from ear to ear moving to the beat of the music.

I cut the song short. I then proceeded to say, "I made a new song last night. Speed and I were up all night writing this song. I had to find the right words for a very special guest that I have here tonight."

Making eye contact with Melissa, I approached her with one rose as photographers took photos. I got on stage and I played my new song. It touched her heart and not only brought tears of joy to her eyes, but two other ladies in the house as well.

That song was a hit. It was my number one on the Billboard chart that made it to the radio and this started the very beginning of my music career.

After the concert, security assisted Melissa to my dressing room backstage. She very gingerly walked in the room.

"So this song; is that you?

Placing my finger on her lips, I said, "That song was for you."

That night, I got my first kiss. What a kiss it was. She kissed me like she was already in love, but she got a hold of herself and said, "Come on, let's get out of here."

We went out the back into my car. She said, "Don't tell me this is your car."

"Okay. I won't tell you. However, I will tell you my name is on the license plates."

She walked to the back of the car. She stared at me and said, "Ya know, you surprised me tonight. No, I mean you really surprised me. I never expected that you were such a gifted person. It's all too much for one girl to take in. You must have many women."

"No, none at all."

"Well, of course you would say that."

"No, really," I said approaching her. "Did you listen to the words in my song?"

"Yes, I did."

"Well, it's for you." I reached in my pocket and gave her an autographed copy.

"Look, I finally got a night out with you and I intend to make the most of it, so shall we go?"

She got in the car and we were off to enjoy the rest of the beautiful night out. She laughed and smiled. She was very happy. Yet, I saw a bit of sadness when it was time to say goodnight.

She said to me, "This was a beautiful night out and your company was very nice. I will always remember it. It's like a dream that only happens once."

It was as if she was saying goodbye forever. "Tell me when you will let me take you out again?" I asked.

"I can't tell you that. You are a star. You are someone who will become one or who already is on his way to fame with the surrounding of women."

"Wait. Hold on just one minute here. I have been singing all of my life. This didn't just happen today. What happened today was what I have been preserving myself for, for years. I am not asking you to marry me, just let it be our beginning. I don't like to categorize people so please don't do it to me."

She slowly turned to me and said, "I'm sorry. I will try not to categorize you. I really enjoyed this night out with you." She laid her head on my chest and said softly, "It was a beautiful night and the song you wrote for me, I will cherish it forever. Then she rose up and kissed me and said good night.

I could hear her when I got in the car because my window was down, saying "Mama, mama! Oh mom, I had the most beautiful night out that I have ever had. I knew then, I was going to make this beautiful lady happy and soon enough she would be mine.

Chapter Five

BLACKOUT

The phone rang. I answered it.

"Speed. What's up?

"Are you still out with your girl?"

"No, I just dropped her off at home."

"You didn't take her home to Granny's?"

"What's up, Dawg?"

"Man, you gotta leave more often and leave me in control because last night, I rocked the house. I was number one!"

Laughing, "Man, did you?"

"Don't tell me you tried to sing."

"No, man."

"You're a liar.

Speed can dance and play music, but he just cannot carry a note.

"Yep, well, I was singing and everybody started laughing and throwing stuff on the stage at me. I whipped out some music and I danced and I jammed on the floor with everybody. I did man. You should have been there. I rocked the house!"

I was driving, talking, and laughing on the phone with Speed. Then all of a sudden, I felt a blow to the head. I screamed so loud, while the phone dropped to the floor, stopping the car from within inches of hitting the center divider on highway 35. I grabbed my head with both hands. I could hear Speed screaming on the other end of the phone.

"T Flow! What happened, Man? Hey. T Flow, are you alright? Answer me, man. You are scaring me. Hey! T Flow? Answer me. What's going on?"

I reached for the phone many times until I finally got a hold of it. My eyes were seeing double and my head was spinning in a circle.

The last words I said were, "Man, I'm down."

My head touched the steering wheel and the horn went off until I was rescued. Not sure who called the ambulance; perhaps, a passing motorist, but when they arrived, the paramedic put something to my nose and that's when I found out I had a stroke of violence in my blood.

When I woke up, I was scared to death with four people staring in my face. I started beating on them. I had no idea what was happening. All I knew was that somebody just hit me in the head and my head was killing me. I had everybody petrified.

When I came out of the frantic state of shock, I asked, "Could someone tell me who just hit me across my head?"

The police officer yelling from behind me said, "Calm down, son. We don't know who hit you. All we know is we found you knocked out cold and your buddy Speed is on his way."

I asked, "Speed?"

"Yes. He was on the phone listening to the car horn waiting for you to get rescued. I could hear Speed saying, "I'm not going to sit there holding the phone waiting for someone to murder my partner." He jumped in his ride with the phone to his ear, circling around from your girlfriend's house to his house looking for you.'"

"Hey, T Flow." Speed gave me the biggest hug straightening up my clothes when he saw me. "You alright, man? You scared me. Don't ever do that again."

"My head, man. It's really killing me."

Speed helped me to his car.

"I'll take you to the crib."

"Uh, excuse us. We don't mean to interrupt, but we need to examine him and transport him to the hospital," one of the ambulance attendants said.

I told Speed to park his car and follow me in my "ride" so he could take me home. Speed smiled.

"Uh. I'm in the driver's seat of your car?"

I never let anyone drive my car, so Speed knew I was badly hurt. Soon as the ambulance truck drove off, I went into a deep sleep with my head throbbing.

Chapter Six

RECORD CONTRACT

Soon as I closed my eyes, I felt and saw the butt of a gun hit me upside my head. I was gangster looking. I had a snake tattoo on my muscle. I had a lot of hair on my face, but it was nicely trimmed even though I looked like I had been through quite a bit.

The blow from the gun left blood gushing out of my head. Then an unknown woman jumped on top of me crying and screaming. "No. No. Help me, please. Somebody call an ambulance!"

She kept crying and screaming, "Baby, hold on. You're gonna be just fine." I did not know who this woman was; she was definitely not Melissa.

And why is this woman calling me baby.

I am not her baby.

The paramedics came in and pulled her off of me. She stood back in the corner of the room as a tall black man was holding her. She was doing some "serious" crying like we were lovers. Then she had nerve enough to jump into the ambulance with me. She held my hand crying all the way to the hospital.

"Hold on, baby. Please just hold on. Don't leave me. Lord, don't take him from me."

This woman just would not give up. She was still frantic at the hospital. They wheeled me into the emergency room where I saw them stitch my head back together and wrap it up in a bandage. Then I fell asleep. When I woke up, I had slept a whole day. It was finally quiet and no one was bothering me. I didn't hear the sound of anyone crying. The nurses periodically came in and out of the room to check on me.

They checked my vitals and wrote on the chart that was on the foot of my bed. When the doctor came in, I could hear him saying, "Get this one undressed. I need to examine him to see if this had anything to do with gang-related activity. I need to give a report to the police if it looks to be so."

When the nurse undressed me, you should have seen my body. It was buffed. Nobody could mess with me, I thought. I had tattoos all over my body.

I don't know why I got so many tattoos,

but I sure like my toned body. And what

was he talking about -- gang related?

Get real.

My body twitched when I heard

that "crying" lady walking into the

room.

"Andre. Baby, I'm here. Andre?"

She's calling me Andre.

"Baby, wake up. You are going to

be fine. You had me so scared there for

a minute. I know you are going to be

just fine now. Doctors said, you might sleep for a while, and I want to jump in bed and lay right beside you, but they won't allow me to do that. Baby, I'm going to be right downstairs. I am not going anywhere until you open your eyes."

Then she stood up looking at me, smiling and shaking her head back and forth. After that, she started to walk towards the door to exit the room, but she glanced at me first. Before she opened the door, she said, "Jacka__."

Then she left.

I was shocked when she said this.

I didn't even know her, so why was she

acting like she loved me? Then called

me a jacka__ under her breath. On top

of that, she called me Andre. She don't

even know me. You crazy b___, I

thought.

My body started to resemble

signs of movement. My arms reached

up to touch my head and my eyes

opened instantly.

"Hey. What the hell is this? Hello? Get in here." I was mad as hell. When the nurse started to walk into the room, she stopped and stood at the door trying to calm me down before approaching me.

"Sir, you have a concussion. Try to stay calm because you can hurt yourself. I will call your doctor to come and speak with you."

"Come over here, lady. What happened? Did I die?"

"No, you were just unconscious. I'll be right back with your doctor."

I was trying to remember what happened and then it dawned on me; there were a lot of people in this house. They seemed to all know me. It looked like we were having a party.

Everybody was "bumping and grinding;" dancing in my living room. They were drinking and rolling blunts (marijuana).

The woman who called me a jacka__ passed by me talking with her girlfriends. I reached down and smacked her on the butt. She turned around and gave me a "sloppy" kiss.

I mean, she was "advertising" it all as she jumped up into my strong muscle arms. I had no choice but to carry her off the dance floor and up into my bedroom. I threw her onto the bed and pulled off my shirt. She had a body that was to die for. You could see that she worked out. There was a tattoo on her body that said Andre.

There came a knock at the door. I said, "Who dat?" No one answered. "I said man give me some privacy. I'll be right out." Just as I put my hands on my pants buckle, the bedroom door was shot opened with a bullet. I picked up my "hottie" and pushed her across the room. I dove for my gun that was in my nightstand next to the bed. When I reached for my pistol, the door flew open.

"Don't even try it, Andre!" The huge guy holding a big gun in his hand was pointing it at me saying, "Let me see your hands, man.

I wasn't too scared because I walked right up to the mouth of his gun and put it to my heart. I said softly, "You gonna shoot me, Bullet? I knew the guy's name. "Shoot me. But you better kill me, man, because you will not live one day pass today."

Bullet said, "Man, where is my money? Then I turned around and walked toward a picture on the wall. I lifted up the picture and a safe was behind the picture.

"Bullet, this is not the proper way to ask for your money. For one, I don't handle my business from my "crib" and never around my girl. Shayla, get out!"

She left instantly through the outside balcony. Then I opened the safe with the gun pointed in my face. I reached inside of it for an envelope that had Bullet name written on it. I quickly closed the safe and handed the envelope to Bullet.

Bullet said, "You are not supposed to avoid my calls."

I said, "What?" I grabbed my phone, but the battery was dead. As I raised my head, the butt from Bullet's gun went across my head. I screamed so loud, "Shayla."

****

"Hey. Baby, how long have I been down?"

"Two whole days."

"Where's Bullet?"

She bent over to whisper in my ear. "A police officer is right outside your door," then she paused. "Bullet has been taken care of."

"I said, "Mmmm. You are the best baby; you know that?"

She said, "Oh yeah." Then she gave me another one of those sloppy kisses.

I said, "No, baby. Not right now."

I lifted the covers and went for my

clothes. I started unhooking all the IV's they had attached to me.

"Shayla, call Pee Wee. Tell him to come and get me now."

Shayla left right out the door and didn't even say goodbye. I screamed, "Shayla!"

She peeked around the door and said, "You ain't got your cell?"

"Yep, but there is no reception in this room."

The police officer who was right outside my door came walking in. I pushed the button for the nurse. She answered on the microphone, "May I help you?" looking down the hall at the police officer with no respect.

"Yes, you can help me."

Then nurse interrupted, "I'll be right there."

"Officer, I need to complete this report." I said.

"Oh. And I guess I'm supposed to help you?"

"Nurse, nurse!" The nurse came running in.

"Yes, sir."

"Get these people out of my room and give me something for my pain."

"Andre?"

I screamed, "Get out!"

The nurse jumped up and said, "Officer, his heart is rising. You need to leave."

The officer walked out saying, "I will be back."

The nurse said, "You unhooked everything? You need to lie down." I laid down as she hooked me back up and gave me two pain pills and some water. I took them and closed my eyes. Then the nurse turned off the lights.

Pee Wee came in five minutes behind her. I jumped up as soon as I saw him.

"Ready?" he asked.

"Help me unhook this."

He unhooked it carefully. I grabbed all my belongings while Pee Wee put a scarf gently over my concussion, then he threw a beanie on me and a jacket. As we walked out of the room; we turned the lights out.

****

I could hear someone calling me by my right name. "T Flow, wake up, man." It sounded like Speed. When I opened my eyes; I was in a hospital bed with sweat pouring down my face. It was Speed standing over me. I was so happy to see him.

Chapter Seven

MOVING OUT

"Speed, I had one hell of a nightmare. How long have I been out?"

"Two whole days. I hope you are well rested and ready man because I got some news for you. First of all, how ya felling, man?"

"Dizzy. My head is spinning. Hey man, did you call Granny?"

"For sure. I got your back, man."

"My car, where is my car?"

"I parked it at the night club in your garage. Man, you're not going to believe this."

"Woe, man--Melissa."

"What about Melissa?"

"Does she know I been down two days?"

"I'm supposed to contact all your one-night stands."

T Flow interrupted, "Man, it's not a one-night stand. I'm not going to trade this beautiful lady in for a hoochie mama named Shayla."

Speed's eyes popped out, "Who is this hoochie mama named Shayla? Wait. Hey, man that song you wrote is taking us to a whole new level." He jumped up saying.

The record producer from R & B Records was in the house the night you played your song.

T Flow jumped up with his eyes glowing. "You a liar!"

Speed hollered. "We are going to the top!

"Would you quit? What are you saying?"

"T Flow, I been trying to get this out since I woke you up, but you won't let me have the floor."

T Flow said loudly, "You got the floor now. What' up?"

"R & B Records wants you and me.

This is why I couldn't let you sleep another day. I unsnapped your Morphine IV, so you would wake up. We got business to take care of T Flow," Speed said, while laughing and dancing.

After he told me this great news, I said, "Let's get out of here. Hand me my cell phone and my clothes."

"Are you alright to leave?" Speed asked. "You need medicine."

"Man, would you quit? If I need medicine, I will send you out for it later. Just get me out of here."

Speed was in the habit of making sure I was decent before making an entrance, so while he was checking me and fixing me up, I was checking my phone messages. I said to Speed, "I need to make a phone call from this hospital to Melissa; I don't want her to have any doubts about me."

Speed said, "Okay." Then he sat down in a chair.

T Flow looked at Speed with his phone in his hand, "Can a man have some privacy?"

Speed left the room. "All I know is that I don't want no hoochie mama, and I'm going to do everything (dialing Melissa's number at the same time) it takes to get her to be mine forever. Melissa is the girl of my dreams, not no Shaniqua, or whatever her name is."

There was a brief silence until she answered the phone. "Hello, Shaniqua? Uh hu...Melissa?" stumbling with my words.

"Oh, no. I blew it," T Flow thought.

Then he heard Melissa say, "You have dialed the wrong number." She quickly hung up. She must have looked at the caller ID because she called right back. I answered, "Hello."

"T Flow?" she said.

"Melissa, where are you?" I explained everything to her about how I took a blow to the head. She wanted to see me right away and started to make her way to the hospital. I told her I was dressed to leave, but she said that I could not leave until the doctor released me. "If you don't get back in the bed and wait for me to come see about you, then I'm calling the hospital to tell on you." she exclaimed.

I hung up the phone and crawled back into the hospital bed. Then I called the nurse so she could hook me back up to my IVs before Melissa got there.

Right after this, Speed popped in the door. He saw the nurse giving me medication. He began to laugh, "Ha…ha…ha…talking so long on the phone that you got busted."

I chuckled and thought to myself, "I guess, I better let him believe it." I told Speed to set an appointment with R & B Records in a few days and to call me later because Melissa was on her way. I told him to also phone Granny to let her know I was awake.

Speed said, "Okay, man. Later." Then he left heading home.

Melissa came in ten minutes after Speed left. When she arrived, the doctor was examining me. She sat at my bedside holding my hand listening to the doctor talk. When the doctor left, she kissed me on my lips and asked, "Are you okay?"

I replied, "Now that you are here, I am fine. Will you have dinner with me tonight?"

She asked, "How are we supposed to do that? I heard the doctor say loud and clear maybe you can leave tomorrow.

I responded, "I will. I just need you to stay with me. I will order us a fantastic dinner. Will you just stay and keep me company tonight? Please say yes. I really missed you."

"Okay, but I have to drop off my school assignment first. I will be back in time for dinner." Then she reached over to kiss me goodbye. I pulled her back for more.

"What time should we order dinner for -- 6:00 p.m.?"

"I will be back at 6:00 p.m. then."

"Okay." I said. Then she left.

I thought about Melissa when she left and how fortunate I was to have a woman like her in my life. How in the world did I get such a wonderful woman like her? Melissa, not only was pretty, but she was smart, too. You see, Melissa was in college studying to be a lawyer. I was so glad to have her in my life.

I couldn't wait for Melissa to come back that night. As soon as she left, I ordered the best food in the city from "Devin's Eatery," along with a chef and his grill.

Then I called Granny and asked her to bring me a change of clothes, so

I could be clean and decent for my hospital dinner date.

Melissa came stepping in right at 6:00 p.m. in a beautiful dinner dress carrying balloons and a get well card.

She was so surprised at how I pulled off such a delicious meal in a hospital room. We laughed and talked all night and played dominoes. Then she laid next to me watching TV until visiting hours were over. Before she left she asked, "Do you want me to pick you up in the morning?"

I said, "No. How about I come to kidnap you in the morning? Tomorrow is Saturday and you have no school or work, right? Can I have you for one whole day?"

"Sure. I will be waiting." Then she kissed me goodbye.

All I could think about was I have to make this girl mine, so when she left, I started unhooking my IVs again and called Speed. I told him to pick me up in 10 minutes. When he came, he had a girl with him. He dropped her off at home after I got in the car.

The next morning, I got up early and went shopping. I wanted to be in the stores, the minute they opened. I wanted to go shopping for Melissa before I picked her up. I wanted to get something special for her.

I didn't think about my music all day because I was so into Melissa. "Today was going to be her day," I said to myself, "And tomorrow we will be there at the studio to celebrate after I sign the contract."

Thoughts kept going through my mind about the crazy dream I had. The part that bothered me the most was that the woman in my dream was not Melissa, so I figured somewhere along the line in our lives, I might have focused too much into my music where I ended up losing her.

Well, I'm not going to let that happen. I know business comes before pleasure, and I do intend to take care of business, but I will always have her somewhere in my daily schedule. So I decided Sunday; I would take her to church with me, but today will be a day just for us.

When I went to pick her up, we engaged in a warm embrace. Melissa always looked pretty no matter what she had on. Only today she was not dressed for the day I had mapped out for us. She had on a whole lot of clothes. It's a good thing I had the whole day mapped out. I handed her a bag and asked her to go and change. She looked in the bag, then looked up at me and smiled and kissed me and said okay.

"I'll be right back. Make yourself at home," I said. I was dying to see how she looked. When she came out of the bedroom, she looked like someone who belonged in a magazine. She started posing as I got my camera and started taking pictures. Then she grabbed the camera and took pictures of me. I took off my shirt and started posing also. Then she yelled for her mom to take a picture of us together.

"Mom, you need to take more than one," Melissa said.

Then her mom asked, "Do you have a bathing suit that can fit me in this bag?" We all laughed.

Looking at Melissa, she said, "You look very pretty, Melissa." After that, we left on our way to start our adventurous day.

When we reached a certain location on our journey, I parked the car and rented bikes from a local vendor. We rode until we reached a boat.

Melissa asked, "Is this yours?"

"No."

"Can you ride this boat?"

"No--well, I can, but I'm not driving it today because someone else will be driving us. I need to focus on you." No sooner than I said that, the driver started the boat and took off to my surprise rendezvous for Melissa.

As we got on our way, we begin to kiss. Then I reached around her neck and clasped a chain on her.

She said, "What is this?"

I said, "It's called a leash."

She smiled and said, "A leash? Like for a dog?"

I said, "No, for my girl." It says, "I belong to T Flow."

"I want to see it," she said.

I grabbed her hand and said, "It looks beautiful on you. You will see it later. We have to catch a fish right now."

I prepared a reel for her and myself. We tossed the fishing poles together in the water and within three minutes, we pulled in a beautiful fish. I prepared it and we cooked it on the stove. We ate and danced until the sun went down.

When the boat stopped at our destination, I reached and gave her a dress and asked her to freshen up. This night I was going to take her out on the town.

I went in one bathroom and she went in the other. She came out and said, "You have very good taste in clothing. And how did you size me so perfectly?"

"That's a man's secret baby. I can't release it."

"If I were to buy you something, I would never be able to guess your size."

Pulling her towards me, I said, "So let's just make a deal while we are young and growing up together; I do all the shopping. When we get older and you beg me to marry you, then you can do all the shopping. Okay?"

She kissed me and said, "No deal. That is not a deal." Then she sat on my lap and looked at my collar size and said, "Medium size."

"Now, would you like to view my pants size?" I said jokingly.

"No," she said smiling at me.

"Let's go because time is getting away from us and you are just fooling around." After she said this, she looked at me crazy. I kissed her on her cheek, pulled her by the hand, and under both our breaths, we started laughing heading toward the rental car I had rented for the night.

We went to Disneyland and had a wonderful time. We got on all the rides especially the roller coasters. I won a great big teddy bear for her. Can you believe it? She won one for me too.

We had to put them in the car because

they were interfering with our evening.

Then we stopped to get a hot dog and

drinks. After I took a bite, I said, "This

has got to be the worst part of our

date."

She looked at me, "What's that

supposed to mean?"

I replied, "This is the nastiest hot

dog I have ever bit into. Can I spit it

out?"

She looked at me laughing. I turned my head with my napkin as I grabbed my hot dog to toss everything in the trash.

"Come on. We need a meal." I said. Then I drove out to a place where they have dinner and jazz with a comedian. I can't remember the name of the restaurant, but the food was delicious.

Melissa seemed to enjoy it as well. As we were finishing up our meals, a lady passed by our table. Then she stopped and said, "My goodness, your necklace is beautiful."

I immediately said, "Thank you." That lady walked away saying, "Ohh...weee. He must love you."

Melissa whispered, "Did I ever tell you thank you?" Then she kissed me and said, "I finally looked at it when I went to the bathroom on the boat. I said, "Oh, my Lord, this is beautiful.'" I said thank you in the bathroom, but I don't know if you heard me. Did you hear me?"

"No, the music was on and I didn't hear anything. Are you kidding me? I mean is she for real?" When I saw her go to the bathroom I knew she was hunting down a mirror, so I went to listen at the bathroom door. I probably could have heard her if I was up on the deck.

After we finished eating dinner, I took her for a ride. Eventually, we parked the car and decided to take a walk. As we walk gazing up at the stars we begin "fussing" and debating which one was Jupiter. She was really happy and we kissed and hugged all night until it was time to take her home. I told her thank you for giving me this day today. I loved her company.

She said, "Thank you. I must say you really know how to show a girl a nice time. You must be a professional at this."

I looked at her. I couldn't tell her that she was my first real date because she would just eat that up. So I just said,

"I'll take it that this might mean that you will be my lady?"

She smiled at me touching her necklace and said, "Looks like its official now."

I hated for this night to end and I got the feeling that she did too. I told her that church service was at 10:00 a.m. tomorrow morning. I asked her if I could come and get her. She said, "Yes."

The next morning, we did go to church, and I must admit it, I really enjoyed it considering I had not been in a while. After church, we went to lunch. Then I had to meet with Speed, so I took Melissa home.

She said she needed to study anyway because she had a test coming up. I took her home and then I went to take care of business with Speed.

Speed and I had an appointment with R & B Records, and that night we signed a contract with them. That night they played my dedicated song to Melissa on the radio. I called and told her to turn on the radio and she was screaming in my ear from excitement.

That night, Speed and I also went out to celebrate. We drank beer and danced all night. I mean it was a celebration to remember. Granny was so excited; she just kept crying and crying.

"I take it she is real proud of me," I said to Melissa when I talked to her on the phone.

It wasn't too long after this that Speed and I moved out of our parents' house and into a more private area. It got to the point that nobody was letting us sleep in their homes. And everyone wanted to come over and congratulate us, which was truly cutting into our sleeping hours. It seemed as though it was a never ending cycle.

Chapter Eight

ENGAGEMENT

n the meantime, as Melissa and I continue to date, we found ourselves growing closer and closer together over time. Then Melissa began to be harassed by people. I guess some people found out that Melissa

147

was my girlfriend and they started invading her privacy also. It was really annoying for her. So I had to get her a place of her own away from the people.

I knew it had to be nice as well as safe. I made sure of this. I also had to pay for her to continue her schooling in a much better school - somewhere closer to her new home. After all, it was my fame interrupting her future plans. I did everything to keep her comfortable, and she was.

She loved her new school and home. She even told me that she wasn't falling in love with me, but that she was very much in love with me. This woman had nerve enough to ask me, "Do you think you will ever feel the same for me as I feel for you?"

I told her, "I try to be careful with love. I try not to get my heart involved because I don't ever want to be heartbroken." I looked at her and she started to cry. She ran to her room and locked the door.

"Melissa. Melissa, open the door."

She told me I should probably leave because she was tired and had a lot of studying to do.

"I guess, you are going to make me talk to you through a locked door?"

I said, "Okay baby, listen. I should have known better. I shouldn't have played with anything like that because I know that a woman is sensitive with the word love. Melissa, I would like to hold you in my arms at the time I tell you how I really feel about you. Baby, open the door."

I heard her unlock the door, but she didn't open it.

"Melissa, isn't it obvious how I feel about you, baby? My Granny taught me ever since I was a little kid that actions speak louder than words."

Melissa finally opened the door. I grabbed her and held her in my arms as tight as possible. "Melissa don't you know I love you. I have loved you since the first day I laid eyes on you. Do you believe in love at first sight?"

"You don't even know a person at first sight," Melissa said.

"Never judge a book by its cover. Okay, at any rate I saw right through you, and you are all I need in a woman, and a whole lot more than what I expected. Also, I have come to realize that there is even more to learn about you as we continue to build a solid foundation.

She said, "Nope, that's about it. There is nothing else you don't know about me. You know everything."

I kissed her and asked, "Everything?"

She said, "Yep. Everything."

I said, in the midst of kissing and caressing her on her bed, "I am sure, I still have more to learn. I need to know you from the top of your head to your feet." I kissed her feet while saying that. I was always afraid of touching her in the wrong way and scaring her off.

After Melissa was calmer, I kissed her good night, then I went home. But I made sure the door was securely locked as I left.

The next morning when I returned, she made me breakfast. I was amazed of how well she could cook. She made homemade pancakes, eggs and bacon.

"You see, I told you there is more to learn about you," I said. "This is delicious and so are you."

Yes, things were going great with

me and Melissa. I even ask her to quit her job, so we could spend more time together, and she did. One good thing for sure, that came out of our record deal was that I was able to take care of all the financial needs for my place and Melissa. When Melissa needed money, I would make sure she had what she need.

I also gave her a credit card, and why not, I had so much cash I didn't know what to do with it all.

However, from time to time, I still needed to hang out with Speed. But sometimes, I would spend so much time with Melissa; Speed looked like he was lost, so at times, he would get wasted. However, he eventually snapped out of this real quick. He had to. During these days, the record company was pressuring us to make more music.

My life was moving so quick because everything was happening at the same time. Melissa had finished law school, and the only thing she had to do is pass the bar. However, I still found some time to take Melissa to Hawaii to celebrate her 23rd birthday. I was so excited because I had planned to propose to her there.

When we got to the island of Waikiki and we went out the first night, I was so nervous when I began to pull the ring out of my pocket and asked her to marry me. I reached across the table and grabbed her hand and said, "Melissa, I love you. There is no other woman I would want to spend the rest of my life with other than you. Will you marry me?"

Melissa looked at me in amazement and said, "No." I couldn't believe she said no. She was so straight-forward. Then she said, "I don't want this beautiful life you have given me to come to an end. If you were to marry me, you will eventually want me to have kids, which I might end up raising them by myself causing my career; perhaps, to be flushed down the toilet.

Do I want to marry you? Yes, but I want to be your wife *for the rest of my life,* not just for a little while. I want it forever. However, we never even discussed marriage, so I must say no now."

I said, "Well, after you say yes, that's when we will start our plans for the future. We will both agree together on our plans; right? Now, Melissa is your answer really no?"

"Yes, yes, yes. I will marry you."

We celebrated and made all our plans and discussed our future the very next day. We slept the whole day away. She said I was tossing and turning in my sleep all night, but I wouldn't wake up. She said it seemed like I was fighting somebody. All I could remember in my dreams is that I was running. Maybe it meant my life was moving too fast. Oh well, I don't know.

During those days, all the music Speed and I were making seemed to hit charts at the top 10. We would be up all hours of the night singing and playing. Eventually, we decided to purchase a bigger house -- one where Melissa could move in and we could be on the other side of the house with our music. Everybody agreed and it was done.

We had a beautiful house and Melissa had plenty to keep her busy. We had two horses, which she loved to ride with her friends. A tennis court, this was her favorite sport. I had me the best exercise gym right at home, a pool table, a sport's bar; everything at my disposal. We even had a maid every day.

Everybody was happy until Speed and I had to break the news to our "girls" that we had to go on tour for three months.

Melissa wasn't having it. "I'm going to be left in this big house by myself. See, that's what I meant by you leaving me all alone to raise kids by myself. I'm not going to do it. I'm going with you."

"Are you sure?" I asked.

"Yes, I can study wherever you go. All I need now is to take my bar exam. I'm going to take it when I know I can pass."

I was so happy to know that my going on tour would not interrupt her goals and that she was able to travel with me.

All of my music that went out on my cd covers never revealed my face because my supporters and fans were always surprised at concerts because I remained a mystery to them, but we

were glad to be touring again.

Chapter Nine

DOUBLE STANDARD

Our last tour performance was in New York. I was on stage and I heard a woman yell the name Andre, which reminded me of my dream awhile back. I will never forget it.

I was singing and everybody was cheering, then all of a sudden out of nowhere, I hit the stage floor as if I was shot. I could barely breathe. I was wheeled into a hospital. I could hear the nurses saying, "He's been shot," but I didn't have any blood. So they must have been talking about the patient who the paramedics just wheeled in. I was in so much pain. I thought I was going to die. I was out cold. I went into a coma and there I was again, dreaming about running. I was running hard with sweat pouring down my face and someone was shooting at me.

I saw myself get shot and throughout the rest of my dream, all I did was stare at myself inside the mirror. Maybe my dreams were messages that I needed to slow down. When I woke up from my dream, in my hospital bed, no one was around. So all I did was think about my dream that made me think about my life.

Maybe I'm working too hard. I don't feel like I'm working too hard.

When I sing and I'm on stage, I'm having fun. So how is it, I'm working too hard? This doctor is going to have to tell me what's going on with my body and then I will go from there. I was just about to call the nurse into my room and a woman came in the door. She threw herself on me saying, "Oh thank. God, you are okay. Then she yelled, "Why did they have to shave off the hair on your face?"

Just then, I remembered this woman from my dream, but I am

awake. Then I heard the voice in the next room yell out.

"Shayla! Where are you?" She starred at me. We both turned to look and see where this voice came from. It was a patient in the room next to me. She went to draw the curtain. We could hear the voice calling Shayla again. The partition was opened and it was as if I was looking in a mirror.

Melissa walked in when everyone was starring and in shock. This man looks exactly like me. And the pain I got on stage is in the exact same spot where he got shot. I got up and walked in his room. I asked, "Would your name happen to be Andre?"

He said, "Is your name T Flow?" We were both shocked. We said, "F___k," at the same time.

He said, "Wait a minute man; this is some crazy! Your girl's name is Melissa?"

"Melissa, yes. Oh my, God. What is all of this? You are studying to be a lawyer?"

She said, "Yes."

"I'm totally shocked." Then I took the floor.

"Did a man by the name of Bullet shoot down your bedroom door just when you and your girl was about to get your groove on?"

"Yep!" Laughing.

"You saw that man? Did you see my girl? My baby gets down." Kissing Shayla while saying it.

"Yep. Well, I see you and your girl."

"Now that's love! I mean, that's real love."

I said, "Well, we are definitely in love. But hold on, man. What is happening? You get hit upside your head with the butt of a pistol and it put me in the hospital. Now, you have been shot and it puts me in the hospital again."

Andre sits up. "No way! Is this real?" Looking at Melissa.

Melissa nods her head, "Yes."

Andre said, "Man, do you sing on stage?"

"I answered, I made the top 10.

What! Andre said. "I'm singing around the house thinking I'm going to be famous one day.

Shayla interrupts, "Yep and I'm always telling him to please shut up because the man cannot sing."

"You be quiet. I can sing." Everybody laughed. "But we are all confused. What is the connection?

Who are your parents? Maybe we are related, cousins, or something."

I said, "Well, probably so. You've got to be right because we definitely are the same. We have to investigate. When you get released, are you free to go back home with me? "

I told Andre, "I would take care of everything and even Shayla could come with you. And I will see to it that you both are very comfortable."

"Man." Andre said. "From what I know about you from my dreams, your word is gold, and we shook on it."

I put Andre and his girl Shayla up in the back house of our home. At one point, I saw Shayla pick up something and attempt to put it in her purse and Andre slapped her hand and said, "One more stunt like that again and I'm sending you back home by yourself. I'm going to see this mystery out all the way through." He whispered in her ear. "He can see what you do in his dreams."

She said, "Well then, don't let him go to sleep.

Andre, Speed, and I sat up all night talking about our life trying to see if names were familiar, but nothing rang a bell for us. We were headed out to see Granny first thing in the morning. Melissa took Shayla shopping.

The morning afterward, we did go to Granny's house. When we arrived, Granny was glad to see me. She was doing laundry, but she immediately stopped to greet me. I told Granny, I need you to meet someone. Granny turned around and fainted. We got her to come to and she fainted again. We looked at each other and said, "Maybe she thinks she is seeing double." I told Andre to go to the kitchen when she wakes up.

Granny woke up. "T Flow, what's happening?"

"I want you to meet someone."

She started crying and said, "I know I saw him where is he? Where is your brother? I'm so sorry, baby. Come here. Let Granny see you." She hugged him saying, "Oh God, thank you. How did you find him?"

I said Granny, "What are you talking about?"

Granny told us all about how our real parents always dressed us alike and how we did everything the same. When our parents died, the courts would only allow her to have one child. She said, "I fought that system for years and when I found someone who could help me, we couldn't find the baby. You had been adopted. Someone took to you immediately."

Andre said, I was never told I was adopted."

Granny said, "What? Maybe that explains why the trail of you was lost. There was a woman handling our case and out of nowhere, the woman, the files, and you just disappeared."

Andre jumped up, "You're liar! You think my mama kidnapped me? No way. Wait a minute. Maybe that's why she always said, "I should have just let that old lady just go on and raise you."

She was always yelling at me, I should have let her have you!" And then she said, "You ruined my life. I had a good life."

"I always thought I was an unplanned early pregnancy.

Andre was so upset. He was about in tears. "This woman ruined my life. I'm a gangster man. I could have had a sweet life like you."

I told him, "We would try to make up for all the time. You can't go back there."

"Why not?"

"Because I feel it in my blood that you would kill her and you cannot. You can call her and confirm, but I will never let you go back there again. We will put her away the right way. Come on, brother; let us go get a drink."

I took Andre out for lunch. We sat in a bar shooting pool and drinking beer. He was still set on going back to settle a couple of scores. I guess, anyone could figure out what that meant knowing he's a gangster and just got shot, and then finding out he was robbed of his glorious childhood with his real family. I could feel his heart was very cold.

I talked all day. "After all these years, we finally got to be around each other. I have a brother, and if you leave, I feel I will never see you again."

He said, "Man, I am coming back."

As strong as he was, I still was able to pin him against the wall. I said, yelling at him, "I can feel your heart and its cold as ice. Let me take care of it the right way!"

He said very calmly, "Man, I could hurt you. You know that's right? Look at my muscles. I'm strong."

I said, "Come on with it. Let's do this. Take your anger out on me, brother. Let's do it."

He laughed. We both started laughing.

He said, "Alright, you win. I'll stay. I'm home now with my real family."

I said, "Now, that's what I want to hear."

On the way out, Andre said, "You know, I can beat you, right?"

I said, "Yep and I want my muscles to look just like yours. I got a weight room at the house. Let's go work out."

My brother Andre and his girl, Shayla, got settled in our home. They sent for their things and decorated the back house. Shayla got a job as an interior designer. She was real good at it.

Melissa finally passed the bar and she could officially become an attorney. Her first job was already mapped out for her and that was to put away Andre's kidnapper. She couldn't wait to get started.

Melissa said, "You know my fees are expensive."

Andre said, "I will sell everything to pay you for this."

"I have a family discount plan, and you'll probably go broke. My fee is one dollar."

She wanted to frame it. She said, she had already been working on the case.

Andre searched around for something he could do, but he was undecided. I noticed he had been outside a lot riding our horses like they were race horses, going faster and faster.

Years ago, I got the horse some gear and I entered him in a contest. In his very first horse race, he won third place. Over time, the horse got better and better. Pretty soon I invested in another horse. He was very happy. Everybody was happy and very busy, seriously into their careers.

Speed and I went to work on new music. Andre kept his word and made no contact with his kidnapper. He didn't want to give her a chance to leave the state. When Melissa presented her case in court, the judge ordered an arrest for this lady. She had no idea what was going on. The day we arrived in the court room, we were 25 years old. She saw us together and cried. I was so proud of Melissa that day. I got to see all that bookworm-studying go to work. She did one hell of a job. We were all proud of her.

The woman was put away for the rest of her life. Before they took her away, Andre stood in front of her and they both looked at each other. He did all he could to refrain himself from hitting her. He didn't say a word. He looked at her with a straight face watching her being led out of the courtroom.

Andre showed us all that he was pleased with his new way of living. Right after Melissa won her first case, her career took off when the media got a hold of the story. My baby was busy, but not too busy to make our wedding plans and never too busy for me.

Melissa and I were married and we went on our honeymoon in Hawaii. When we got back, Andre and Shayla went to Las Vegas for a week and while they were there, they got married also. Speed said, maybe, it's time for him to move out because he didn't want the girl that he was seeing to get any ideas. He said marriage was just not for him.

Speed had many women all the time and he could never be still or serious about just one girl. This one time when I was appearing in Chicago, we all were able to go. It was snowing and we made plans to play in the snow after our first performance. I had just started rapping on stage, and Melissa, Andre, and Shayla were back stage coming around to the front.

The stage was quiet, and I started the music for my next song. I blew Melissa a kiss and over the music, I hear someone yell real loud, "Andre!" I was shot. Andre turned around and saw the man who shot me leaving in a hurry. They all came up to be with me and we all went to the hospital. I went into a deep sleep and I saw myself dead. They couldn't bring me back to life. I saw Andre, all my friends, and my dear sweet Melissa pregnant crying her heart out. I saw my funeral and watched Andre scare the man that killed me and eventually shoot him down till the gun was empty.

After this incident, I saw the rest of my brother's life being good and happy. Melissa had two twin boys and she brought them to lay on my grave faithfully. Melissa always felt that whether we were together or apart, I was always with her and I was.

To order more copies, please visit:

Amazon.com or
www.deborahbroadyministries.org

198

About the Author

Deborah Jeanne Broady was born August 6, 1960 to Richard and Augusta Broady in Chicago, Illinois. Deborah was the middle child of seven: 3 brothers and 3 sisters. Deborah's family moved to California when she was five years old where she lives today.

Deborah attended Fullerton high school and Fullerton JC. She was married at age 21 divorced at age 25, and married again at age 36. But by the age 39, she was divorced again. Deborah has three gorgeous children:

Desiree C. Greer, Fhedale A. Wallace, and Devin Orange.

Deborah worked all her life supporting two children with no child support. Yes, it was a very tough road for her as a single parent; yet, in the end, God gets all the glory, because she survived it all.

Deborah has also been blessed with a talented granddaughter who is pursuing her dream as a basketball scholar, Delacey L. Brown. As Deborah continues her 31 years working for the U.S. Postal Service, she looks forward to writing a sequel to this book.